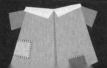

For Mom and Dad

Copyright © 2007 by Janee Trasler

Little, Brown and Company

Hachette Book Group USA
1271 Avenue of the Americas, New York, NY 10020

Visit our Web site at www.lb-kids.com

LB kids is an imprint of Little, Brown and Company Books for Young Readers,
a division of Hachette Book Group USA. The logo design and name,
LB kids, are trademarks of Hachette Book Group USA.

First Edition: August 2007

LCCN: 2006933215

ISBN: 0-316-06530-7

10 9 8 7 6 5 4 3 2 1

Printed in Singapore

Little **Boo!** Books

Ghost Gets Dressed!

Janee Trasler

LITTLE, BROWN & COMPANY
LB kids™
NEW YORK BOSTON
lb-kids.com

Ghost wears a hat.

Monster wears the hat.

Ghost wears a coat.

Monster wears the coat.

Ghost wears mittens.

Monster wears the mittens.

Ghost wears a scarf.

Monster wears Ghost!